Disney · PIXAR INSIDE OUT

GUIDE to LIFE

randomhousekids.com
ISBN 978-0-7364-3559-8
Printed in the United States of America
10 9 8 7 6 5 4 3 2 1

Disney · PIXAR
INSIDE OUT GUIDE to LIFE

By Courtney Carbone

Random House 🏠 New York

Life can sometimes be **chaotic.**

Things don't **always** go your way.

Maybe you feel **stuck** in the same place.

Or that you've lost something important to you.

Don't throw
a tantrum ...

or lose your head . . .

Focus on the good things!

Look for the **fun** all around you!

March to the **beat** of your own drum.

Don't try to be just like everyone else.

Be **confident** in your journey.

Friends and loved ones will **carry** you through.

Don't let new **opportunities** pass you by!

You might feel as if others
are **holding you back** . . .

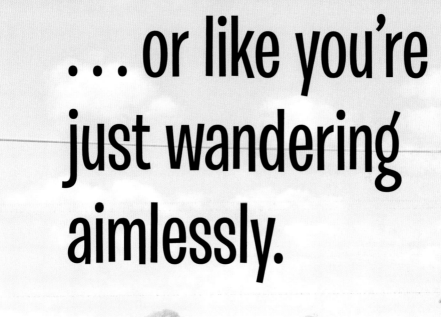

... or like you're just wandering aimlessly.

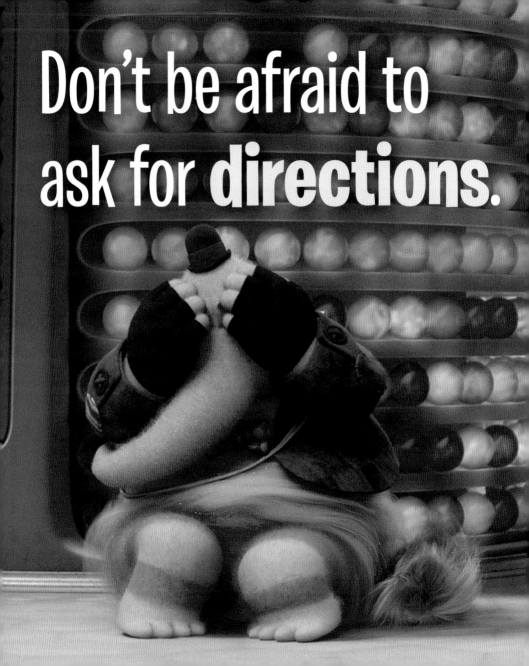

Someone will show you the way!

Big changes can be **overwhelming.**

But you will get through.

Don't be scared to try **new things.**

Look for **adventure!**

Every day is a **chance**
to make new memories ...

and **new** friends.

Remember the past and **celebrate** how far you've come.

Don't put too much **pressure** on yourself!

Do what you can with the cards you've been **given**.

Think **happy** thoughts!

Appreciate the beauty all around you.

It's normal to have **good** days . . .

and **bad** days.

Don't let **Fear** get the best of you.

The whole world is not against you.

There are lots of people on your side!

Give yourself
a break!

SUGAR COATED
CARAMEL
CORN
CURLS

FREE

Enjoy life's simple pleasures.

Let yourself play!

Life can be
a bumpy ride!

But we're all in the same **boat**.

Everyone gets scared sometimes.

Be brave and face your fears.

Finding the right path is not always easy.

There's no instruction manual
to tell you what to do.

Trust the **guidance** of those who have been there before.

They know what it's
like to be in your shoes.

Start every day with a positive attitude!

And end every day with a good bedtime **story**.

Trust that everything will work out.

EDITORIALS

Why does everything smell funny?

EXTRA The Mind Reader EXTRA

FUTURE IS SHAKY!

And remember —
have **fun**
along the way!